Grandpa's Too-Good Garden

by JAMES STEVENSON

GREENWILLOW BOOKS, *New York*

FOR PETE

Watercolor paints and
a black pen were used
for the full-color art.
The text type is
ITC Clearface.

Greenwillow Books,
a division of William
Morrow & Company, Inc.,
105 Madison Avenue,
New York, N.Y. 10016
Printed in Hong Kong by
South China Printing Co.
First Edition
10 9 8 7 6 5 4 3 2 1

Library of Congress
Cataloging-in-Publication Data

Stevenson, James (date)
Grandpa's too-good garden
by James Stevenson.
p. cm.
Summary: Grandpa tells
Mary Ann and Louie about
a garden he had years ago
that his brother Wainey
"helped" him plant.
ISBN 0-688-08485-0.
ISBN 0-688-08486-9 (lib bdg.)
[1. Gardens—Fiction.
2. Grandfathers—Fiction.
3. Humorous stories.
4. Cartoons and comics.]
1. Title.
PZ7.S84748Gae 1989
[E]—dc 19
88-18776 CIP AC

"Hello, Louie! Hello, Mary Ann!" said Grandpa.
"Gardening, eh? What fun!"
"It's not, Grandpa. It's awful!" said Mary Ann.
"We dig and rake and plant and water and weed—
   and nothing ever comes up! Our garden is no good,"
   said Louie.
"Maybe that's just as well..." said Grandpa.

"It was a long time ago," said Grandpa.
"One warm day in April I started a
little vegetable garden in the backyard.
I planned where I'd put all the
vegetables, and I started to dig.

I was having a grand time until…"

"I gave him easy things to do.

I tried to teach Wainey about gardening.

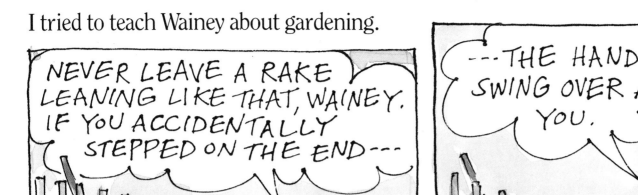

THIS IS A HOE, WAINEY.
YOU CHOP WITH THE HOE, LIKE THIS---
CHOP. CHOP.
FUNCH!
WAINEY HOE.
?

After a few days, the garden began to look pretty good. I put out strings.

At last it was time to plant.

We planted the garden and watered it."

"Did your vegetables come up, Grandpa?" asked Mary Ann.
"No, indeed," said Grandpa. "Weeks and weeks went by...

We began to get desperate.

Finally we gave up."

"That night, something strange happened.

Wainey and I went to bed.

During the night it rained very hard. The next morning we looked out the window."

"Had the garden grown?"
asked Louie.

"A lot," said Grandpa. "It
was taller than the house.

We ran up and down the rows.

We pulled up some vegetables...

and had salad for lunch.

After lunch we took a nap. When I woke up . . .

Wainey had climbed high up on a plant and was bouncing on the leaves.

When I tried to stop him,

Wainey fell off a leaf."

"That was lucky," said Mary Ann.
"Not really," said Grandpa.

"It was an enormous caterpillar.

The caterpillars ate all the vegetables— including the plant I was on."

"I was fortunate enough to get snagged
on a weather vane above our roof.

In a few minutes the caterpillars were gone, and there wasn't a leaf left in the garden.

My parents were quite upset."

"How did you get down?" asked Mary Ann.

"I didn't," said Grandpa. "I was up there all night. Toward morning I must have fallen asleep because I woke to a strange sound!"

Overnight, all the caterpillars had turned into butterflies.

Wainey came by on one of the butterflies and rescued me."